# Fairy Cooking

## Rebecca Gilpin and Catherine Atkinson

Designed by Nicola Butler
Illustrated by Molly Sage
Photographs by Howard Allman

## Contents

# Spangly heart biscuits

To make about 25 biscuits, you will need:

2 tablespoons caster sugar
pink food colouring
75g (3oz) butter, softened
3 tablespoons light soft brown sugar
3 tablespoons maple syrup
1 medium egg
175g (6oz) plain flour
a medium and a small heart-shaped cutter
two greased baking trays

Heat your oven to 180°C, 350°F, gas mark 4.

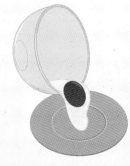

✿ The biscuits need to be stored in an airtight container and eaten within a week.

Add one spoonful of maple syrup at a time.

1. Put the caster sugar in a bowl, add two drops of colouring and stir the sugar until it is pink. Then, spread it out on a plate to dry.

2. Put the butter and soft brown sugar into a large bowl. Stir them hard until they are creamy, then stir in the maple syrup.

3. Carefully break the egg into a small bowl, then pour it slowly onto a saucer. Then, put an egg cup over the yolk.

Keep the egg white.

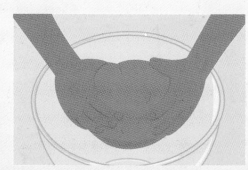

4. Hold the egg cup over the yolk and carefully tip the saucer over the small bowl so that the egg white dribbles into it.

5. Add the yolk to the large bowl and mix it in. Sift in the flour and stir it in well, then squeeze the mixture to make a dough.

6. Wrap the dough in plastic foodwrap and put it in the fridge to chill for half an hour. While it is in there, heat your oven.

7. Sprinkle a clean work surface with flour. Then, use a rolling pin to roll out the dough until it is about 5mm (¼in) thick.

8. Use the medium cutter to cut out heart shapes. Then, lift the hearts onto the baking trays with a fish slice.

9. Cut holes in the hearts with the small cutter. Then, make the scraps into a ball, roll them out and cut out more hearts.

10. Using a fork, stir the egg white quickly for a few seconds. Brush some onto each biscuit, then sprinkle them with pink sugar.

Wear oven gloves.

11. Bake the biscuits for 10-12 minutes, until they start to turn golden brown. Then, carefully lift them out of the oven.

12. Leave the biscuits on the baking trays for a few minutes. Then, lift them onto a wire rack and leave them to cool.

# Pretty fairy fudge

To make about 70 fudge shapes, you will need:

450g (1lb) icing sugar
100g (4oz) pink marshmallows
2 tablespoons milk
100g (4oz) unsalted butter
half a teaspoon of vanilla essence
red food colouring
small cutters
small sweets, for decorating

✿ The fudge needs to be stored in an airtight container
in a fridge and eaten within a week.

1. Sift the icing sugar through a sieve into a large bowl. Make a small hollow in the middle of the sugar with a spoon.

2. Using clean scissors, cut the marshmallows in half and put them in a small pan. Add the milk, butter and vanilla essence.

3. Gently heat the pan. Stir the mixture every now and then with a wooden spoon until everything has just melted.

4. Pour the mixture into the hollow in the sugar. Mix everything together until it is smooth, then mix in a drop of colouring.

5. Leave the mixture to cool for 10 minutes, then make it into a flattened round shape. Then, wrap it in plastic foodwrap.

6. Put the fudge mixture in a fridge for three hours to go firm. Then, sprinkle a little icing sugar on a clean work surface.

7. Roll out the fudge with a rolling pin until it is about 5mm (¼in) thick. Then, use the cutters to cut out lots of shapes.

8. Squeeze the scraps into a ball, then roll out the ball and cut out more shapes. Then, decorate each shape with a sweet.

To make 'white' fudge, use white marshmallows and don't add any food colouring.

# Fairy muffins

To make 10 muffins, you will need:

300g (10oz) plain flour
2 teaspoons baking powder
150g (5oz) caster sugar
1 lemon
50g (2oz) butter
225ml (8 fl oz) milk
1 medium egg
100g (4oz) seedless raspberry jam
a 12-hole muffin tin
small sweets and sugar strands, for decorating

For the icing:
175g (6oz) icing sugar
2 tablespoons lemon juice squeezed from
the lemon from the main mixture

Heat your oven to 200°C, 400°F, gas mark 6,
before you start.

✿ The muffins need to be stored in an airtight container
and should be eaten on the day you make them.

Use a pastry
brush.

If you are having
a birthday party,
you could decorate
some of the muffins
with little candles.

1. Brush some oil in ten of
the muffin holes. Then, cut
a small circle of baking
parchment to put in the
bottom of each hole.

2. Sift the flour and baking
powder into a large bowl.
Add the caster sugar, then
mix everything together
with a metal spoon.

*Use a lemon squeezer.*

*Heat the pan gently.*

3. Grate the rind from the lemon using the medium holes on a grater. Then, cut the lemon in half and squeeze the juice from it.

4. Put two tablespoons of juice on one side, for the icing. Then, cut the butter into pieces and put it in a pan with the lemon rind.

5. Add four tablespoons of milk and heat the pan until the butter melts. Then, take it off the heat and add the rest of the milk.

6. Break the egg into a cup and mix it well with a fork, then stir it into the butter mixture. Then, add the mixture to the bowl.

7. Stir everything together with a fork. Then, nearly fill each muffin hole with the mixture and bake the muffins for 15 minutes.

8. Leave the muffins in the tin for three minutes, then loosen them with a blunt knife. Then, put them on a wire rack to cool.

*Use a sharp knife.*

9. Turn each muffin on its side and cut it in half. Then, spread jam on the bottom half and lay the top half on top.

10. Sift the icing sugar into a bowl and mix in the lemon juice. Then, spoon icing onto the muffins and press on some sweets.

# Swirly pink biscuits

To make about 40 biscuits, you will need:

75g (3oz) icing sugar
150g (5oz) butter, softened
1 lemon
200g (7oz) plain flour
2 tablespoons milk
pink food colouring
two greased baking trays

Heat your oven to 180°C, 350°F, gas mark 4.

The biscuits need to be stored in an airtight container and eaten within a week.

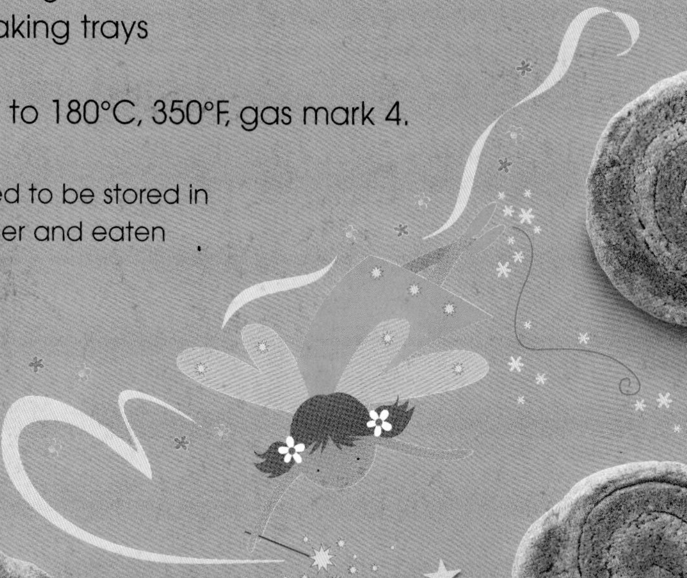

1. Using a sieve, sift the icing sugar into a large bowl. Add the butter and mix it in until the mixture is smooth and creamy.

2. Grate the rind from a lemon using the fine holes on a grater. Then, add the rind to the creamy mixture and stir it in.

3. Put half of the mixture in another bowl. Sift half of the flour into each bowl, then add a tablespoon of milk to each one.

4. Add three drops of colouring to one of the bowls. Then, squeeze each mixture to make two balls of dough.

5. Flatten the balls of dough a little and wrap them in plastic foodwrap. Put them in the fridge for 30 minutes to chill.

6. Sprinkle flour on a clean work surface, then roll out the plain dough until it is about 25 x 15cm (10 x 6in) and 5mm (¼in) thick.

7. Roll out the pink dough until it is about the same size as the plain dough. Then, brush the plain dough with a little water.

8. Carefully lift the pink dough and lay it on the plain dough. Then, use a sharp knife to make the edges straight.

*The layers of dough make a spiral when you roll them.*

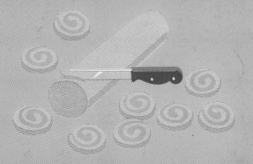

*Use a fish slice.*

9. Roll up the dough from one of the long sides. Then, wrap it in plastic foodwrap and chill it in the fridge for 30 minutes.

10. Turn on your oven. Then, cut the rolled-up dough into 5mm (¼in) slices and put the slices on the baking trays.

11. Bake the biscuits for 12-15 minutes. Leave them on the baking trays for two minutes, then lift them onto a wire rack to cool.

# Mini fairy pastries

To make 24 pastries, you will need:

375g (13oz) packet of ready-rolled puff pastry
1 medium red onion
1 tablespoon of olive oil
half a teaspoon of dried mixed herbs
a pinch of salt and of ground black pepper
150g (5oz) mozzarella cheese
12 small cherry tomatoes, washed
1 tablespoon of milk
2 baking trays

Heat your oven to 220°C, 425°F, gas mark 7, before you start.

❀ Leave the pastries to cool for five minutes, before you eat them.

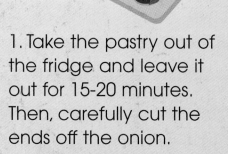

1. Take the pastry out of the fridge and leave it out for 15-20 minutes. Then, carefully cut the ends off the onion.

2. Peel the onion and cut it in half. Then, cut each half into two pieces. Very carefully cut each piece into thin slices.

3. Gently heat the olive oil in a frying pan. Then, add the onion and stir it every now and then for about five minutes.

4. Remove the pan from the heat and stir in the herbs, salt and pepper. Then, unroll the pastry and cut it into 24 squares.

5. Put the squares on the baking trays, leaving spaces between them. Prick the middle of each square twice with a fork.

6. Open the mozzarella bag and pour away any liquid. Cut the mozzarella into tiny cubes. Then, cut the tomatoes in half.

7. Pour the milk into a mug. Then, brush milk around the edge of each square, making a border about 1cm (½in) wide.

8. Spoon some of the onion and herb mixture onto each square, making sure you don't cover the milk border.

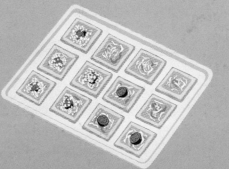

Use a fish slice to remove them.

9. Put half a tomato on the top of each square, then scatter a few cubes of mozzarella on top of each one.

10. Cook the pastries for 12-15 minutes. When the edges have risen and gone brown, the pastries are cooked.

# Pretty fairy star biscuits

To make about 25 biscuits, you will need:

350g (12oz) plain flour
2 teaspoons ground ginger
1 teaspoon of bicarbonate of soda
100g (4oz) butter
175g (6oz) soft light brown sugar
1 medium egg

4 tablespoons golden syrup
writing icing
small sweets, for decorating
a large star-shaped cutter
2 greased baking trays

Heat your oven to 190°C, 375°F, gas mark 5, before you start.

✿ The cookies need to be stored in a single layer in an airtight container and eaten within five days.

1. Sift the flour through a sieve into a large bowl. Then, sift the ginger and bicarbonate of soda into the bowl too.

2. Cut the butter into chunks with a blunt knife. Then, add it to the bowl and stir it in so that it is coated with the flour.

3. Rub the butter into the flour with your fingers until the mixture is like fine breadcrumbs. Then, stir in the sugar.

4. Break the egg into a small bowl, then add the syrup. Beat them together well with a fork, then stir the mixture into the flour.

5. Mix everything together until you make a dough. Then, sprinkle a clean work surface with flour and put the dough onto it.

6. Using your hands, push the dough away from you and fold it over. Do this again and again until the dough is smooth.

7. Sprinkle more flour onto the work surface, then roll out the dough until it is 5mm (¼in) thick. Use the cutter to cut out stars.

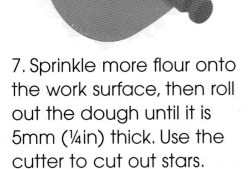

8. Lift the stars onto the baking trays. Squeeze the scraps into a ball, then roll them out again and cut out more stars.

The cookies will be golden.

9. Bake the biscuits for 12-15 minutes. Carefully lift them out of the oven and leave them on the baking trays for five minutes.

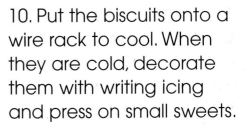

Stick on single sweets with a dot of icing.

10. Put the biscuits onto a wire rack to cool. When they are cold, decorate them with writing icing and press on small sweets.

# Flowery cut-out biscuits

To make about 10 biscuits, you will need:

100g (4oz) butter, softened
50g (2oz) caster sugar
a small orange
1 medium egg
2 tablespoons ground almonds*
200g (7oz) plain flour

1 tablespoon of cornflour
8 tablespoons seedless
  raspberry jam
a 5cm (2in) round cutter
a small flower cutter
2 greased baking trays

Heat your oven to 180°C, 350°F, gas mark 4, before you start.

✿ The biscuits need to be eaten on the day you make them.

*Don't give these biscuits to anyone who is allergic to nuts.

1. Put the butter and sugar into a large bowl. Mix them together with a wooden spoon until the mixture looks creamy.

2. Grate the rind from the orange using the medium holes on a grater. Then, add the rind to the bowl and stir it in.

3. Break the egg into a cup and mix it with a fork. Then, add a little of the egg to the creamy mixture and mix it in well.

4. Add some more egg to the bowl and mix it in. Carry on until you have added all the egg, then add the ground almonds.

5. Sift the flour and cornflour into the bowl. Then, mix everything with your hands until you have made a dough.

6. Wrap the dough in plastic foodwrap and put it in a fridge to chill for 30 minutes. While it is in there, heat your oven.

7. Sprinkle some flour onto a clean work surface. Then, use a rolling pin to roll out the dough until it is about 3mm (1/8in) thick.

8. Using the round cutter, cut out lots of circles. Then, use the flower cutter to cut holes in the middle of half of the circles.

9. Squeeze the scraps into a ball. Then, roll out the ball and cut out more circles. Put all the circles on the baking trays.

*The biscuits turn golden brown.*

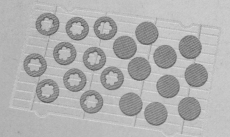

10. Bake the biscuits for 15 minutes. Leave them on the baking trays for two minutes, then move them onto a wire rack to cool.

11. Spread jam on the whole biscuits, as far as the edge. Then, place a flower biscuit on each one and press it down gently.

# Tiny fairy cakes

To make about 24 fairy cakes, you will need:

1 medium egg
50g (2oz) self-raising flour
40g (1½oz) soft margarine
40g (1½oz) caster sugar
small paper cases
a baking tray

For the icing:
50g (2oz) icing sugar
about 1 tablespoon of warm water
pink food colouring
small sweets and sugar strands, for decorating

Heat your oven to 180°C, 350°F,
gas mark 4, before you start.

✿ The cakes need to be stored in
an airtight container and eaten
within four days.

Use a wooden spoon.

1. Break the egg into a
mug. Then, sift the flour
into a large bowl and
add the egg, margarine
and caster sugar.

2. Stir everything together
well, until the mixture is
smooth and creamy. Then,
put 24 paper cases on
the baking tray.

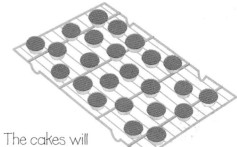

The cakes will
turn golden brown.

3. Using a teaspoon,
spoon the cake mixture
into the paper cases until
each case is just under
half full.

4. Bake the cakes for
about 12 minutes, then
carefully take them out of
the oven. Lift them onto a
wire rack to cool.

The fairy cakes are a little smaller than the ones shown here.

5. For the icing, sift the icing sugar into a bowl. Add the water and mix it in with a metal spoon until the icing is smooth.

6. Spoon half of the icing into another bowl. Then, add two drops of food colouring to one of the bowls and mix it in well.

7. Using a teaspoon, put a little icing onto the top of each cake. Then, use the back of the spoon to spread out the icing.

8. Decorate the cakes with small sweets or sugar strands while the icing is still soft. Then, leave the icing to set.

# Iced raspberry mousse

To make 4 mousses, you will need:

150g (5oz) raspberries
4 tablespoons icing sugar, sifted
4 tablespoons Greek-style yogurt
150ml (¼ pint) double cream
25g (1oz) meringues*
fresh raspberries and small mint leaves,
  to decorate
four 150ml (¼ pint) ramekin dishes

❀ The mousses need to be stored in a freezer and eaten as soon as you have decorated them.

1. Put the raspberries in a bowl and mash them with a fork until they are squashed. Then, add the icing sugar to the bowl.

2. Stir the raspberries and icing sugar to mix them. Then, add the yogurt and stir it in until everything is mixed together.

*If you can't find meringues in the shops, you can make your own (see pages 28-29).

3. Pour the cream into a bowl. Then, use a whisk to whisk the cream until it is thick and there are points when you lift the whisk.

4. Add the yogurt mixture to the cream. Then, gently turn the mixture over and over with a spoon, to mix everything together.

5. Carry on until the whole mixture is pink. Then, break the meringues into small pieces. Add them to the mixture and stir them in.

6. Spoon the mixture into the dishes. Then, put the dishes into a freezer for two hours, or until the mousses have frozen solid.

7. Take the frozen mousses out of the freezer. Then, decorate each mousse with a raspberry and two mint leaves.

# Cut-out sandwiches

To make 3 sandwiches, you will need:

6 slices of bread
butter or margarine
thin slices of ham
a cucumber
strawberry, raspberry or apricot jam
a large round cutter and a small cutter

✿ Eat the sandwiches as soon as you've made them,
or wrap them in plastic foodwrap and store them in
a fridge for up to six hours.

## Ham sandwich

1. Lay a slice of bread on a chopping board. Place the round cutter on it and press hard. Then, remove the cut-out circle.

2. Cut another circle from a second slice of bread. Then, use the small cutter to cut a shape in one of the circles.

3. Lay the round cutter on top of a slice of ham. Then, very carefully cut around the cutter with a sharp knife.

4. Spread butter on one side of each bread circle. Then, lay the ham on the whole circle and lay the circle with the hole on top.

If you're having a party, make lots of sandwiches in different shapes and with different fillings.

# Cucumber sandwich

# Jam

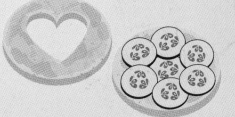

1. Cut two bread circles and cut a hole in one of them. Then, slice the cucumber until you have lots of thin slices.

2. Spread butter on the bread circles and lay slices of cucumber on the whole one. Then, lay the circle with the hole on top.

Cut two bread circles and cut a hole in one of them. Spread butter and jam on the whole one, then press the circles together.

# Chocolate cobweb cookies

To make about 18 cookies, you will need:

160g (5½oz) plain flour
2 tablespoons cocoa powder
100g (4oz) butter, refrigerated
50g (2oz) caster sugar
2 tablespoons milk
white writing icing
a 6.5cm (2½in) round cutter
2 baking trays lined with baking parchment
a toothpick

Heat your oven to 180°C, 350°F, gas mark 4.

✿ The cookies need to be stored in a single layer in an airtight container and eaten within five days.

1. Sift the flour and cocoa into a large bowl. Cut the butter into chunks and add it to the bowl, then rub it in with your fingers.

2. When the mixture looks like fine breadcrumbs, stir in the sugar. Then, sprinkle the milk over the mixture and stir it with a fork.

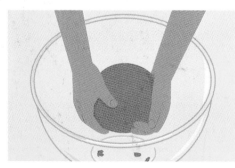

*Make a squashed circle.*

3. Stir the mixture until everything starts to stick together. Then, squeeze it with your hands to make a ball of dough.

4. Wrap the dough in plastic foodwrap and put it in a fridge for 20 minutes. While it is in there, heat your oven.

The flour stops the dough sticking.

5. Sprinkle a clean work surface and a rolling pin with some flour. Then, roll out the dough until it is about 5mm (¼in) thick.

6. Use the cutter to cut out lots of circles and carefully lift them onto the baking trays. Then, make the scraps into a ball.

Wear oven gloves.

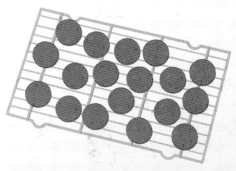

7. Roll out the ball and cut out more circles. Bake the cookies for 10-12 minutes, then carefully lift them out of the oven.

8. Leave the cookies on the baking trays for about five minutes. Then, lift them onto a wire rack and leave them to cool.

9. Draw a spiral of white writing icing on each cookie, starting in the middle and working out towards the edge.

10. Using a toothpick, drag the icing from the middle to make a web. Ice the other cookies then leave the icing to set.

# Butterfly cakes

To make 8 cakes, you will need:

1 medium egg
50g (2oz) self-raising flour
quarter of a teaspoon of baking powder
50g (2oz) caster sugar
50g (2oz) soft margarine
paper cake cases
a baking tray with shallow pans

Heat your oven to 190°C, 375°F,
gas mark 5, before you start.

✿ The cakes need to be eaten on
the day you make them.

For the butter icing:
40g (1½oz) butter, softened
a few drops vanilla essence
75g (3oz) icing sugar, sifted
about 4 teaspoons seedless
   raspberry jam
extra icing sugar, for dusting

1. Break the egg into a
mug. Then, sift the flour
and baking powder into a
large bowl. Add the caster
sugar, egg and margarine.

2. Stir all the ingredients
together with a wooden
spoon. Carry on until you
have made a smooth
creamy mixture.

3. Put eight paper cases
into the pans in the
baking tray. Then, use a
teaspoon to half fill each
case with the mixture.

4. Bake the cakes for 16-18 minutes. Then, carefully lift them out of the oven and put them on a wire rack to cool.

Wear oven gloves.

5. To make the icing, put the butter into a bowl and add the vanilla. Stir them together until the mixture is really creamy.

Use a wooden spoon.

6. Add some of the icing sugar to the butter and stir it in. Repeat this until you have mixed in all the icing sugar.

7. Using a sharp knife, carefully cut a circle from the top of each cake. Then, cut each circle in half, across the middle.

Leave an edge around the circle.

8. Spread some of the icing on top of each cake. Then, spoon half a teaspoon of jam in a line across the icing.

9. Gently push two of the half slices into the icing, so that they look like butterfly wings. Then, sift a little icing sugar over the top.

# Little cheese scones

To make about 16 scones, you will need:

40g (1½oz) Cheddar cheese
175g (6oz) self-raising flour
half a level teaspoon of baking powder
a pinch of salt
25g (1oz) butter
100ml (4 fl oz) milk
milk, for glazing
4cm (1½in) round and heart-shaped cutters
a greased baking tray

Eat the scones
as they are or cut
them in half and spread
them with a little butter.

Heat your oven to 220°C, 425°F, gas mark 7, before you start.

✿ Eat the scones warm or store them in an airtight container
and eat them within three days.

1. Grate the cheese using the medium holes on a grater. Then, sift the flour, baking powder and salt into a large bowl.

2. Cut the butter into small pieces and add them to the bowl. Then, rub them in until the mixture looks like fine breadcrumbs.

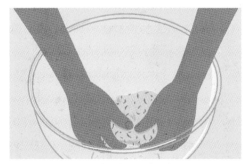

3. Mix in the grated cheese with your hands and pour in the milk. Then, use a blunt knife to mix everything together well.

4. Gently press the mixture together with your hands to make a soft dough. Then, sprinkle flour onto a clean work surface.

5. Using a rolling pin, roll out the dough until it is about 1cm (½in) thick. Then, use the cutters to cut out circles and hearts.

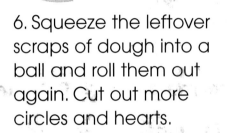

6. Squeeze the leftover scraps of dough into a ball and roll them out again. Cut out more circles and hearts.

7. Put the shapes on the baking tray, leaving spaces between them. Then, brush the tops of them with a little milk.

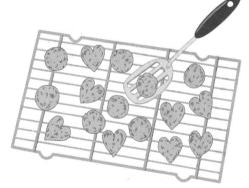

8. Bake the scones for seven to eight minutes, until they have risen and turned golden. Lift them onto a wire rack to cool.

*Some of these scones had a little plain flour or grated cheese sprinkled onto them, before they were baked.*

# Mini meringues

To make about 15 white and 15 pink mini meringues, you will need:

2 eggs, at room temperature
100g (4oz) caster sugar
pink food colouring
150ml (¼ pint) double cream
2 baking trays, lined with baking parchment

Heat your oven to 110°C, 225°F, gas mark ¼, before you start.

❀ The meringues need to be stored in an airtight container and eaten within a week. Once you have filled them, eat them on the same day.

*You could use a yolk to make confetti cookies (see pages 30-31).*

1. Carefully break one egg on the edge of a small bowl, then pour it slowly onto a saucer. Put an egg cup over the yolk.

2. Hold the egg cup over the yolk and tip the saucer over the bowl so that the egg white dribbles into it.

3. Repeat these steps with the other egg, so that the two egg whites are in the bowl. You don't need the yolks in this recipe.

4. Whisk the egg whites with a whisk until they are really thick. They should form stiff points when you lift the whisk up.

5. Add a heaped teaspoon of sugar to the egg whites and whisk it in well. Repeat this until you have added all the sugar.

6. Scoop up a teaspoon of the meringue mixture. Then, use another teaspoon to push it off onto the baking tray.

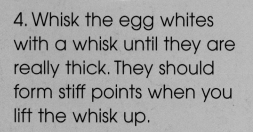

Use a metal spoon.

7. Make 15 meringues, leaving gaps between them. Then, add four drops of food colouring to the rest of the mixture.

8. Gently mix in the food colouring by turning the mixture over slowly. Then, when the mixture is pink, make 15 more meringues.

9. Put the meringues in the oven and bake them for 40 minutes. Then, turn off the oven, leaving the meringues inside.

10. After 15 minutes, carefully lift the baking trays out of the oven. Leave the meringues on the trays to cool.

11. Pour the cream into a small bowl, then strongly whisk it with a whisk. Carry on until the cream is quite thick.

12. Using a blunt knife, spread some cream on the flat side of a meringue. Then, press another meringue on the top.

# Confetti cookies

To make about 100 cookies, you will need:

50g (2oz) butter, softened
75g (3oz) caster sugar
1 egg yolk
1 teaspoon of clear honey
1 teaspoon of vanilla essence
2 teaspoons milk
100g (4oz) plain flour
25g (1oz) cornflour
2 greased baking trays
small cutters

For the icing:
150g (5oz) icing sugar
2 tablespoons warm water
pink food colouring

Heat your oven to 180°C, 350°F, gas mark 4, before you start.

❀ The cookies need to be stored in a single layer in an airtight container and eaten within three days.

The cookies are slightly smaller than the ones shown here and the recipe makes lots of them.

Use a wooden spoon.

1. Put the butter and sugar into a large bowl. Beat them until they look creamy, then add the egg yolk and beat it in.

2. Stir in the honey, vanilla essence and milk. Sift the flour and cornflour into the bowl, then start to mix everything with a spoon.

3. Then, use your hands to squeeze the mixture until you make a ball of dough. If the mixture is a little dry, add a drop of milk.

4. Sprinkle a work surface with flour, then roll out the dough until it is about 5mm (¼in) thick. Use the cutters to cut out shapes.

5. Put the shapes onto the baking trays. Then, squeeze the scraps into a ball, roll them out again and cut out more shapes.

The cookies turn golden brown.

6. Bake the shapes for six to eight minutes, then carefully lift them out of the oven. Leave them to cool on the baking trays.

7. To make icing, sift the icing sugar into a bowl and mix in the water. Then, spoon half of the icing into another bowl.

8. Cover one bowl with plastic foodwrap to stop it drying out. Then, mix two drops of food colouring into the other bowl.

Use a blunt knife.

9. Spread half of the cookies with white icing. Then, spread the others with pink icing and leave the icing to set.

# Marzipan toadstools

To make 8 toadstools, you will need:

250g (9oz) 'white' marzipan*
red food colouring

❂ The toadstools need to be stored in an airtight container and eaten within three weeks.

1. Cut the block of marzipan in half. Then, wrap one half in plastic foodwrap and put the other half in a small bowl.

2. Add three drops of colouring to the bowl and mix it in with your fingers. Then, break the marzipan into eight pieces.

3. Roll each piece into a ball, then squash them to make toadstool shapes. Press your thumb into the bottom to make a hollow.

Wash your hands first.

4. Unwrap the other half of the marzipan. To make spots, break off a third of the marzipan and roll it into lots of little balls.

5. Press several little balls onto each toadstool. Then, break the remaining piece of marzipan into eight pieces.

6. Roll each piece between your fingers to make a stalk. Then, press a red top onto each stalk to complete the toadstool.

* Marzipan contains ground nuts, so don't give the toadstools to anyone who is allergic to nuts.

Series editor: Fiona Watt   Art director: Mary Cartwright   Photographic manipulation: Emma Julings
First published in 2003 by Usborne Publishing Ltd., Usborne House, 83-85 Saffron Hill, London, England. www.usborne.com Copyright © 2003 Usborne Publishing Ltd.